The Coffee Shop

Kerri-Ann T. Thomas

AuthorHouse™ LLC
1663 Liberty Drive
Bloomington, IN 47403
www.authorhouse.com
Phone: 1-800-839-8640

Published by AuthorHouse 01/13/2013

ISBN: 978-1-4918-4569-1 (sc)
        978-1-4918-4570-7 (e)

Library of Congress Control Number: 2013923427

authorHOUSE®

The
Coffee Shop

Kerri-Ann T. Thomas

"A lot of new people in this neighborhood sure do like them some coffee," I said, staring out the window at the coffee shop that used to be a bodega. Today we are moving because our rent keeps going up, and we can no longer afford to live in our apartment.

"Mama, how come the bodega turned into a coffee shop? Didn't the bodega sell coffee?"

"Good question, Clarisse, good question," Mama replied. But whenever she says that, she doesn't answer my question.

"Did you get all your things packed?" she said instead.

"Yes, just about," I said, placing my toy unicorn into a box.

"We should be settled in our new place in no time," Mama said, trying to help me finish.

"Are we moving to those nice buildings up the street?" I asked.

"The new condos? Oh, baby, I wish, but no," Mama replied.

"Mama, isn't there a coffee shop near those nice buildings? Do people really drink that much coffee?"

"Good question, Clarisse, good question."

"Besides, I think chocolate milk is better."

Mama was right, we definitely didn't move into those nice buildings but we made the best out of our new apartment. That is until …

"We have been living here for only three months, and the landlord already wants to meet with me," I heard mama explain to someone on the phone.

Knock, knock! Before the third knock, Mama pushed me into my room and hung up the phone.

"Hello, Ms. Johnson. I know you noticed the new developments in the neighborhood."

"Yes, the boutiques, restaurants, pet shops, and bike shops."

"And coffee shops," I chimed in.

"Clarisse Johnson, get your butt back in your room!" Mama screamed. I went to my room but peeked out of my door so I could see what was happening.

"The owner of some of those new developments wants to renovate our building and is offering the residents money to move out," said the landlord.

"Move out?" Mama's eyes looked like they were going to pop out of her head.

"Yes, the owner is offering everyone good money. But, of course, you don't have to. It's just something to think about," he said, walking out as he headed to a neighbor's door, but not before handing Mama a piece of paper with lots of numbers on it.

"Hey, Mom, why would someone want to pay us for someone else to live *here*?" I asked, looking at the paint hanging off the walls, a window that doesn't shut, a toilet that doesn't flush….*plop!* and a leaky roof.

"Good question, Clarisse, good question," Mama said, staring at the numbers on the paper.

I guess Mama liked whatever she saw on the paper because a week later we were getting ready to move......*again*!

"Your Uncle Rick is on his way to help us move, so try to pack as much as you can," she explained.

Two hours later, Uncle Rick arrived.

"What took you so long?" Mama asked Uncle Rick.

"I stopped to get us some coffee down the block. The line was long. Guess it's a grand opening or something," Uncle Rick said, handing Mama a cup. "Remember when we were growing up in this neighborhood? It used to be called *The Wal*, short for *Walton*."

"I sure do. Now it's called *Walton Hills*," Mama sighed, looking down the block at the grand opening of the coffee shop.

"Cheer up, sis. Even though the name has changed, it doesn't change the history of this place or our memories."

"Mama, would we have to move if the neighborhood was still called *The Wall?*"

"Good question Clarisse, good question," she replied, sipping her coffee. A few hours later, we were in our new apartment.

The move wasn't so bad because a lot of our old neighbors moved too. I guess they didn't like *Walton Hills* or coffee either. Ms. Jenkins is one of those neighbors, and she comes over all the time to talk to Mama.

"Yes, Chile, they pushin' us further to the south," Ms. Jenkins sang. Since she's originally from North Carolina, it sounds like she's singing when she talks.

"I don't know how much more moving I can take and constantly pulling Clarisse out of school. The district zone changes is becoming too much." Mama said.

"Girl, they tradin' in pit bulls for poodles and plastic for paper," Ms. Jenkins added as she slapped her knee.

I don't know who was pushing us, but I didn't want to ask Mama because I would get in trouble for being nosy again. Besides, I don't like pit bulls or poodles.

I didn't like getting used to a new apartment, school, and friends because I was always afraid I would have to move again. So far, we have been living in this neighborhood for about six months and there is not one coffee shop in sight. For some reason, the move felt different this time.

"Hi, I'm Amy!" exclaimed the new girl that was introduced to the class this morning. She didn't seem shy for being a new girl.

"Hi, I'm Clarisse," I said back, trying to finish my lunch.

"I just moved into the neighborhood," Amy explained.

"Do you have a poodle?" I asked.

"No," she said.

"Okay, then we're cool."

Amy and I did everything together. We went to school together and played in the new playground. I loved sleepovers at Amy's. When Mama worked late, Amy's mom, who is a food taster, would always bring us to the new nearby diner where we could sit and eat outside.

One day after school, Amy and I decided to take a short cut home. Amy pointed out a big sign. It said *Coming Soon*.

"Oh, I hope it's an arcade!" she exclaimed.

"I hope it's a dance studio!" I said, just as excited.

Amy ran to the sign to read it more closely. "Aww man, it's just a stupid coffee shop."

I stood there, silent.

"What's wrong, Clarisse?" Amy asked, noticing I was no longer excited. "Are you sad it's not going to be a dance studio?"

"No, it's not that. I just know that I'm moving soon," I said, missing her already.

"Moving?!" Amy exclaimed "When? Where? Why? You can't go! You're my new best friend!" Now we were both sad.

When I got home, I started to pack. Mama walked into the room while I was folding my clothes.

"What are you doing?" she asked.

"Packing," I said calmly.

"Why are you doing that?" she asked, chuckling.

"There's a new coffee shop coming soon in our neighborhood, so I know we are going to move again," I explained to her.

Mama looked at me confused. "Well, actually, that's why I wanted to come home early today. I have good news. I got a promotion at my new job, so it looks like we're staying here for a while."

"Really?!" I asked cheerfully. I couldn't wait to tell Amy.

"Yup! Go get ready so we can go to that diner you like so much," Mama told me.

"Can we sit outside?" I asked.

"Good question, Clarisse, good question," Mama said, winking. And just like that, we were staying and so was the coffee shop. Besides, Mama likes coffee too.

KERRI-ANN T. THOMAS was born and raised in Brooklyn, New York. She received her Bachelor of Arts degree from Spelman College in Atlanta, Georgia and her Masters degree in Education from Columbia University, Teachers College. As an educator, she pushes her students to believe that "although you are a product of your environment you do not have to become a duplicate of the majority." She hopes to inspire not only children through her books, but adults as well, for when you see things through the eyes of a child, you embrace the simplicity of life.

Printed in the United States
By Bookmasters